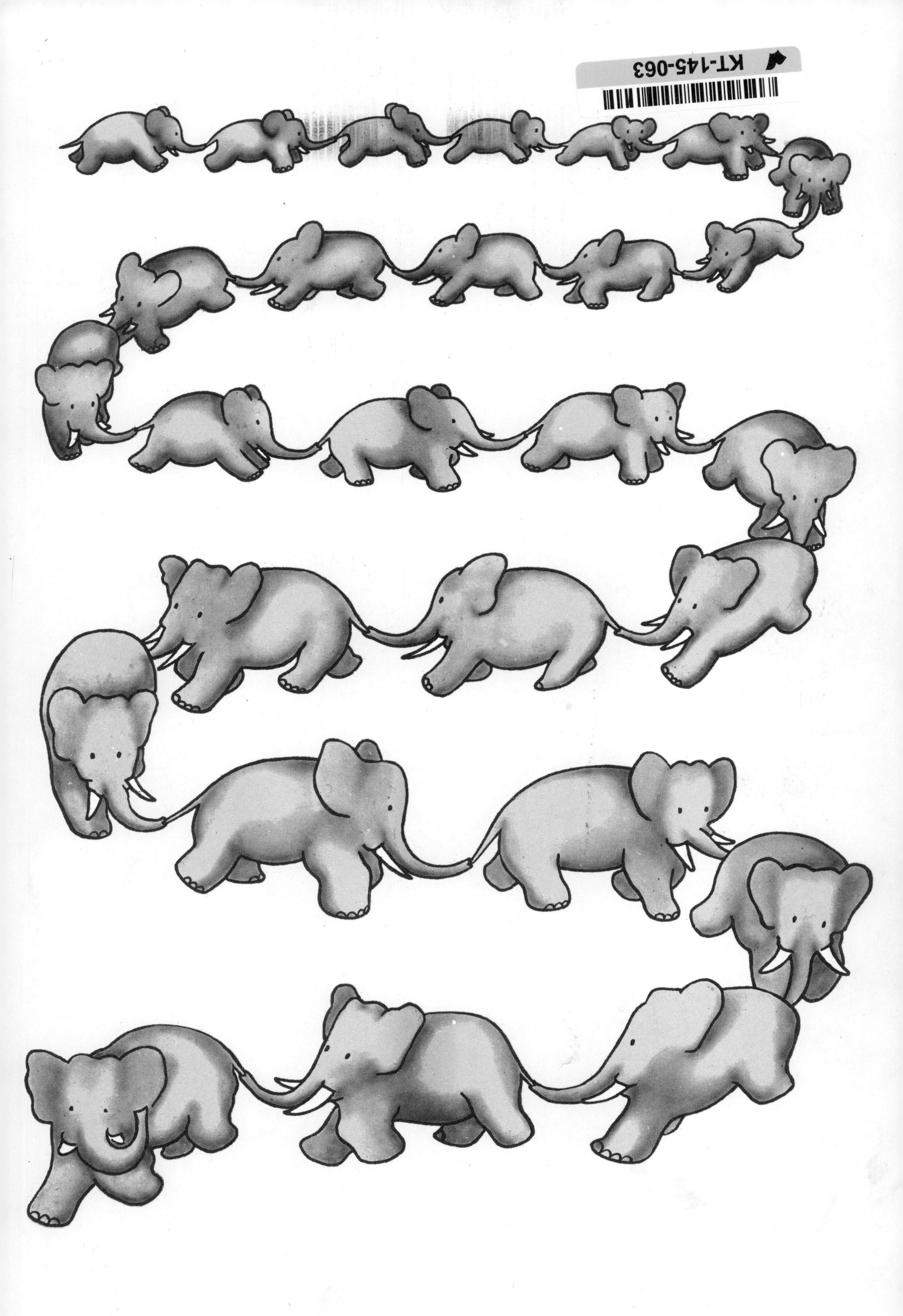

First published in Great Britain 1992
by Methuen Children's Books,
a division of Reed International Books Ltd.,
Michelin House, 81 Fulham Road, London SW 3 6RB.

Printed in the U.S.A.

ISBN 0 416 18696 3

BABAR'S BATTLE

BY LAURENT DE BRUNHOFF

Methuen Children's Books

In Celesteville, the elephants had been living happily for a long time. They had been at peace with their neighbours, the rhinoceroses, ever since King Babar's famous victory over them many years before.

One lovely day Babar and Celeste, his queen, were out for a walk with their children. Babar started thinking about the rhinoceroses and their leader, the cruel Rataxes.

"The rhinoceroses haven't bothered us for a long time," he said.

"No," said Celeste, "but I don't trust them. Rataxes has caused trouble before, and he could again."

Celeste was right.

Unbeknown to the elephants, Rataxes had for some time been under the spell of a sorceress named Macidexia. He visited her often in her underground cavern. She disliked Babar and urged Rataxes to overthrow him.

"You must take your revenge for his victory over you all those years ago," she said. "Babar thinks he is a great leader, but you must prove that you are greater. Invite him to dinner, as though you were friends, and then kidnap him."

"That's a good idea!" exclaimed Rataxes. "I'll invite him immediately."

Babar and Celeste received the invitation for a friendly dinner at Rataxes' palace. As they dressed for the evening, Babar said, "A friendly dinner! Perhaps he has changed his ways."

"Maybe he is trying to deceive you," replied Celeste. "Be careful."

And so, with their friend, Cornelius, Babar and Celeste went to have dinner at Rataxes' palace.

The dinner was a great success. The chef prepared a dozen delicious dishes, and the elephants ate to their hearts' delight.

Rataxes enjoyed himself so much that he completely forgot

about giving the sign to seize the guests. His soldiers, who were waiting to jump on the elephants and take them prisoner, waited in vain for the signal.

Late that night Rataxes saw the elephants to their car. Everyone felt wonderful after such a glorious feast.

"Next time you will come and dine with us in Celesteville!" said Babar as he drove off.

Rataxes descended the path to the grotto. He had promised Macidexia he would come as soon as dinner was over to give her the details of the ambush.

"What am I going to tell her?" Rataxes asked himself as he walked farther and farther down to Macidexia's grotto.

“You idiot!” screamed Macidexia. “You had the chance to get rid of Babar forever.” She spun around with fury, then stopped and faced him squarely. “But I have another good idea.

Empty the lake at Celesteville! Without water, the elephants will be at our mercy."

Rataxes was afraid of Macidexia and ashamed of his failure to seize Babar, so he gave the order to empty the lake.

The rhinoceros engineers installed a powerful pump in a hidden spot to drain the water out of the lake. Immediately the water began flowing into the neighbouring valley and out to sea. A company of guards stood nearby to keep an eye on the pump.

The water level sank rapidly. The creatures who lived in the lake were confused. The flamingos asked the ducks what was happening, the ducks asked the frogs, the frogs asked the fish.

At the palace, when Celeste began to run Isabelle's bath, no water came out of the tap. Isabelle found that amusing, but Celeste was worried.

"What will become of us if there is no more water?" she asked herself.

The gardener was upset too. There was no way to water the flowers. "How dry it is this year!" he said to the children. "The lake has never sunk so low before."

The elephants were in despair to see their once-beautiful lake all dry. There was nothing left but a few puddles. What would they do without water?

Babar, Cornelius and Arthur met to discuss the situation.
"I am sure Rataxes is behind this," said Arthur.
"You may be right," said Babar. "Celeste thinks so too."

Pom, Flora, Alexander and little Isabelle had fun walking barefoot in the mud.

On one of their walks they discovered the pump, hidden under some branches, and realized that it was being used to drain the lake. Just then a rhino guard came running out of the bushes. "Keep away!" he shouted.

Babar spoke to Rataxes on the phone. "Why are you doing this?" he said. "Have you gone mad? I thought we were friends."

"You think you are a great leader, but I will show you that I am greater. My army will meet you at dawn, and this time *I* will be victorious."

With a heavy heart, Babar understood that he had to prepare for war.

The next morning at sunrise, Babar went to see the field of battle. His soldiers had worked hard all night to oil and shine their armour.

"Cornelius," he said, "I have been thinking. I wish to avoid

a war. Instead I will challenge Rataxes to a battle just between the two of us."

"But Babar, what if you are beaten?"

"Do not worry, Cornelius. I have a plan which I am sure will not fail."

Rataxes insisted on having the sun behind him so that it would shine in Babar's eyes and put him at a disadvantage. But Babar had known Rataxes would do this and he was prepared.

When Rataxes charged, Babar raised his shield and sent the ray of sunlight streaming back into Rataxes' eyes. The rhinoceros kept running towards Babar, even though he was dazzled.

Blinded by the sun, Rataxes crashed headlong into a tree and was stuck fast. He thrashed about but could not free himself. Babar's plan had worked.

The elephant gardener cut down the tree and freed Rataxes. The unhappy rhinoceros tried to make excuses.

"It isn't my fault!" he said. "Macidexia made me do it!"

He was sorry for what he had done and wished he hadn't listened to her.

Macidexia returned to her grotto, screaming and stamping her feet. She shook the columns so hard that they cracked. With a thundering roar, the grotto fell in on top of her. She would never cause trouble again.

A few days later some heavy rain fell on Celesteville, and the lake filled up little by little.

How beautiful the lake is now! It seems even more beautiful than before. Everyone wants to go on forever diving, splashing and swimming in the cold, clear water.

And from that day forth, the elephants and the rhinoceroses lived in peace together.

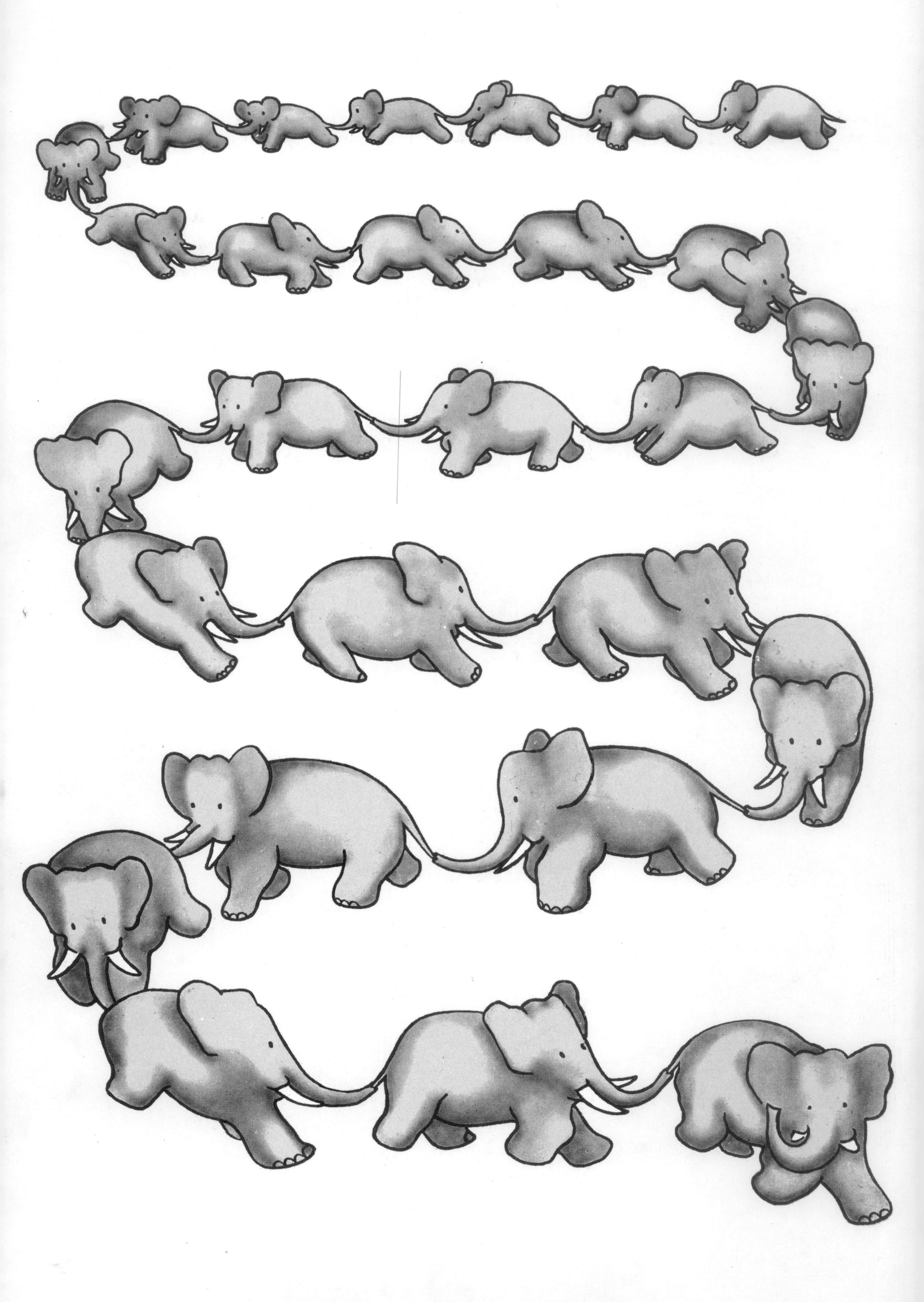